Fifty Wise Words
And
Some Wise Aphorisms—
Sort Of

Fifty Wise Words and Some Wise Aphorisms

ISBN 978-0-9896731-8-1

WmJoy Press is an imprint of Alma Pistis Communications, LLC
WmJoy Press and the WJP logo are trademarks belonging to Alma Pistis Communications, LLC.

PRINTED IN THE UNITED STATES OF AMERICA

Editor's Note

Several Years ago, only God knows for sure, Butch Robertson suggested that he, Steve Wise, and I start the *Friday Lunch Bunch*, which is not an official name. We have no official name; Charlotte LaFever dubbed us the *He-Man Woman Haters Club*, ala the original *Little Rascals*.

It was to be an opportunity for us to get together every Friday away *Church Street United Methodist Church*, usually the only place we saw each other. After just a few times, Henry Naff became member four; a short time later we exploded into between a lot more.

The format was appropriately simple—every Friday, some location, same time. Come if you can. Even I could keep up with that. Current membership is 16; attendance is fluid.

Our first gathering place was *Panera Bread* in Bearden. As we grew *Panera* became too small. So, we moved across the parking lot to *Ruby Tuesdays* where we remained for several years until it closed. The correlation between the two was never determined. The next long-term location fell to, perhaps *upon* is a better word, *The Gourmet Market*, which acceded to *Jason's Deli*, and then on to our current Club House, *Fieldhouse Social*. In between the long-term *clubs* were a few interlopers who couldn't cut the mustard (pun intended). *Big Fatty's* immediately comes to mind.

Not long after all of this began, Wise became the self-appointed secretary/scribe of our little group; a position he takes quite seriously, plus it gives him a sense of purpose. He's the only one who sees it that way.

Every Thursday we received, and still do, a reminder about lunch, which he refers to as *Dinner*—I don't remember why and never understood it anyway. The reminder was an essay of sorts. There is no thematic significance to his essays-just whatever was on his mind at the moment he fired up his computer. Some are only a few lines, others go on for pages. I am particularly fond of his *History of Mullets*. I'm particularly fond of his in depth, pithy analysis of random obituaries of unknown decedents in the *Knoxville News-Sentinel*. It does trouble me that he reads every word of everyone.

COVID-19 abruptly stopped the Friday Lunch Bunch; we descended into deep, dark depression and languished in the loss of lies and laughter (forgive the hyperbolic alliteration). Throwing caution to a slight breeze, we resumed on the patio of Fieldhouse Social in late spring, 2021.

Now that Wise has completely retired from *Shistering*, our scribe is back at it. However, his messages have become *Aphorisms* and *Existential Metaphors* clad as discussion topics. The irony is thick.

The pages that follow are the *Wise Words* and *Wise Aphorisms* that link all of us *He Man Woman Haters* together. They are edited only for format. Spacing is off in some place; I'm digitally challenged. So, TS! I have deleted anything that required prior-to-publishing approval to avoid lawsuits. I may be missing a few but I'm sure 99% of them are here. I hope you enjoy them as much the second time as the first.

I wish to thank Jennifer and Paige at *FedEx Office* in Fountain City for helping me get *Wise Words* print ready, and my publisher, *Imgram Publishing*, for doing this for me expeditiously.

SER

2023

For Steve Wise, my dear friend and one of the three charter members, in celebration of his 70th birthday.

For Butch Robertson, also my dear friend, who stared it all;

And

For the rest of us who look forward to Friday lunch, where we share bread, stories, lies, laugh at each other and ourselves, and rejoice in the common bond of true friendship.

Fifty Wise Words—

Wise Word 1

To a degree not experienced since the first half of the 19th century, we find our society struggling with divisiveness, anger and separation. Ill temper clouds judgment, and the need to prevail over our real or perceived opponents trumps any reasoned approach to problem solving: This compulsion to conflict permeates every corner of our lives:

Arab versus Jew

Red State versus Blue State

Main Street versus Wall Street

Screaming head on cable TV news channel versus Screaming head on cable TV news channel

Leno versus Conan

Lane Kiffin versus First time caller, long time listener

Spleen versus Kevin

In spite of this dismal portrait, from time to time there emerges a spark of insight and truth upon which all reasonable men agree, and in celebration of the subject's 97th birthday next Monday, I proffer the following universal truth which NO man will dispute:

It's hard to find a good Danny Kaye movie.

You will have an opportunity to expose more universal truths at LUNCH (DINNER), tomorrow at 11:50 o'clock AM, the Gourmet Market nestled in the beautiful, cozy, convenient, historic and conflict-free District Village of the Bearden Village District. Suitable attire only.

Wise Word 2

A special called meeting of the Lane Kiffin Fan Club, featuring a presentation by John Adams, Sports Editor of the Knoxville News-Sentinel, along with LUNCH will be held tomorrow at 11:51 o'clock AM, at the Gourmet Market, nestled in beautiful, convenient, trendy and ever-loyal Village District of the District of Bearden Village. Athletic supporters requested

Wise Word 3

You are exhorted: "Fear not the Chief Meteorologists, their assorted Braves and Squaws, their Doppler Radar, their awesome "Storm Team", and their tales of woe! Venture forth! What are you...man, or otherwise?" And pick up some milk, bread, and toilet paper while you are out.

If you are without 4-wheel drive...take a bicycle, but always exhibit courage in the face of the threatening storm...

And since you are out anyway, you are invited to DINNER (LUNTCH) tomorrow at 11:49 o'clock AM, at the Gourmet Market ("Where the truly brave dine"), nestled in the beautiful, convenient, trendy, and tropical Bearden District Village of the Bearden District.

Steve Hillis, lately returned from Terra Incognita beyond the southern 65th latitude will regale you with his recitation of the epic alliterative poem "The Perfidy of Being Pecked by Penguins". Also, the good Dr. Roberts is back, rested and ready

Wise Word 4

As Mr. Larkin reminded the more pious of us on Sunday, this month (February 8) marks the one-hundredth anniversary of the founding of Boy Scouts of America, due to the foresight and efforts of Mr. W. D. Boyce of Chicago, and to the growth of the progressive movement during the early part of the 20th century. As a former Scout myself (Cub and Boy), I can attest to the importance of Scouting in helping to shape an adequate citizen out of an otherwise dubious youth. Plus, you get to go camping.

There are at least three Eagle Scouts among our assemblage, and perhaps more. I, unfortunately, did not achieve Eagle rank, but my momma promised me that I could be special in other ways.

In a related matter, there are reports that Ken Wise and Bob Woodson, (both of whom celebrated birthdays this week), have made competing applications to the Chehote District of the Great Smoky Mountain Council of the Boys Scouts to be recognized as the OLDEST LIVING EAGLE SCOUT in the world.

Bob's application relies substantially upon his prized Copper Chipmunk Award, purportedly awarded for 116 years of continuous service to the organization. The provenance of the award is uncertain, and inquiries are being made to substantiate the claim.

Ken's application acknowledges that Bob has an earlier date of birth, but insists that Bob's sad, lonely existence cannot accurately be construed as LIVING. The analysis continues, with an announcement of the decision planned for Scouting's Sesquicentennial Celebration.

Be Prepared to offer your insights tomorrow at DINNER (LUNCH) at 11:54 o'clock AM in the recently renovated Baden-Powell Room of the Gourmet Market, nestled in the trustworthy, loyal, helpful, friendly, courteous, kind, obedient, cheerful, thrifty, brave, clean, and reverent Chehote District of the Bearden Village District of Bearden

Wise Word 5

I am embarrassed to admit that we let the passage of the King's birthday pass earlier this year, without appropriate note or celebration.

Elvis, who left the building for the last time on August 16, 1977, at the shockingly young age of 42, would have been 75 years old on January 8. Amazing...how old am I, anyway?

I note with some pride that I got to see the King perform (during his dotage period) at Stokely Athletic Center, a few months prior his demise.

Conspiracy theories and mystery stories about the King's death have flourished for years, sparked most likely by the rather unfortunate situs of his passing. It appears that the definitive word on the matter has at last been writ by Elvis' personal physician, Dr. George Nichopoulos of the Memphis medical community, who now, some 33 years after the fact, announces that the King died from chronic constipation. Who knew?

Based on Dr. Nichopoulos' findings, my brother Ken asserts that he has already had three near-death experiences this year.

Al Gourmet, deputy chef and bookkeeper of The Gourmet Market and Grocery, wants to assure each of you that the menu offered tomorrow at LUNCH, at 11:51 o'clock AM, will be neither binding nor restricting, and hinted that some of the available desserts may have a modest loosening effect. Bon Appetit

Wise Word 6

Could it be?!!? The fair State o Tennessee has at long last been designated by a national media outlet as NUMBER ONE. After dwelling in the cellar in every category imaginable, including school funding, graduation rates, teen pregnancy, meth labs, literacy, support for the arts, and number of teeth per mouth, Tennessee has now been identified as Number One in Public Corruption by the web paper "The Daily Beast." Huzzah and Hurray.

Far be it from me to question anything found on the internet, but I cannot see how we could beat out New Jersey where 3 sitting mayors, 2 state assemblymen, 5 Rabbis, and 34 others were indicted on some goofy massive money laundering scheme, or worst yet, Illinois, where every Governor's swearing-in ceremony is followed immediately by an indictment. Blagojevich alone should put the Land of Lincoln over the top.

Irregardless, I have been comforted and assured by Al Gourmet, deputy chef and beekeeper at the Gourmet Market and Apiary, that LUNCH will be served corruption free to all who will partake at 11:54 o'clock AM on Friday (not tomorrow...Al couldn't make any promises about Thursday).

Wise Word 7

I noted with great interest this week's email message which Mr. Lefever circulates for the Parables Sunday School class. For those of you not on that list, Jim, acting in his role as Commissar-for-Life, has decreed due to the coming of Labor Day, coupled with the broken air conditioner, that coats and ties should no longer be worn by the men in the class. He also included some sartorial suggestions for the women which seems a bit risky to me.

Since he has not worn a coat for more than the proverbial "month-of-Sunday-Schools", but still wanting to share in the spirit of the new standards, Butch has announced that he will appear this and following Sundays without pants. He will, however, continue to wear a fashionable belt to keep his shirt crisp and tidy, and to display his girlish figure.

Upon learning of these developments, Al Gourmet, Chief Deputy Chef and seamstress for the Gourmet Market and Dress Shoppe, has revised the upcoming specials menu. The all new "Butch Plate" will feature a bottomless salad bowl and moon pies.

You will be able to enjoy that repast and many others tomorrow at LUNCH at11:49 o'clock AM in the Gourmet Market and Store, nestled in beautiful downtown Bearden Village.

Wise Word 8

Ohio, the Buckeye State, is a strange place indeed, at least this week. Never in a million years would one anticipate that a big game hunt featuring lions, tigers, bears, wolves (and even a herpes-ridden monkey, for Pete's sake) would take place in a small town in Ohio. Yet less than 90 mile away, up I-70, we find an unsavory group of "rogue Amish" terrorizing their neighbors.

OK...which is goofier: (1) a marauding monkey with herpes, or (2) a rogue Amish farmer? This is not a rhetorical question.

I tend to go with the rogue Amish guys, because their approach to terror is to shave the beards off of their neighbors using battery powered clippers. I'm not sure which is more chilling, the involuntary beard removal, or the use of an electric devise. My world view of the Amish is completely upended.

The best part of the story is that 2 of the culprits who have now been apprehended, are Johnny Mullet and Lester Mullet. And their bond was posted by Sam Mullet. Perfect...

The Mullet, as a fashion statement, has been around a long time. Contemporary writers from 6th century Byzantium, note that local rebels would wear the peculiar haircut ("business in the front, party in the back"), apparently patterned after the fashion of the Massgeteans, an Irani nomadic confederation from the 4th Century, which the 6th Century Byzantines referred to as the Huns.

The next known sighting of a Mullet, in the early 1960, is believed to on the head Soon the trend spread, and Mullets were found on the heads of entertainment luminaries as Florence Henderson and Michael Bolton. And then, of course, into the general population.

Beyond the Amish, the Mullet has also found a religious significance. *Mullet b* is the declared god of *Religion b*, a satanic cult derived from obscure math text books. *Mullet b*, according to legend, walks the earth today, and is supposed to be endowed with the world's worst Mullet, but has never been photographed. Artist's renderings of *Mullet b* are reported to have killed 7 Japanese tourists off the coast of Bognor Regis, a seaside resort town in West Sussex on the south coast of England. I swear, I don't make this stuff up.

In September of 2003, a local radio station, "The River-100.3", began a promotion encouraging its listeners to allow representatives at Tennessee School of Beauty to cut off their Mullets. In a remarkable show of edginess, the UT Daily Beacon fought back against the promotion, announcing a campaign to "Save the Mullets". Beacon writer Leslie Wylie argued that asking a Tennessean to cut off his (or her) Mullet would be akin to directing the people of Florida to go out and run over all of the manatees with their boats. I am not sure I understand the logic of that argument, but I love the imagery.

Not unlike the Dude, the "Mullet abides", and I believe that I am OK with that. Knowing that somewhere out there a Mullet is walking around, I am strangely comforted that in spite of all of my shortcomings and failures, I am better than somebody.

You are encouraged to share your hairiest stories and sartorial advise tomorrow at LUNCH (DINNER) at 11:52 o'clock AM at the Gourmet Market and Hair Salon, in beautiful downtown Bearden. Food will be served.

Wise Word 9

NASHVILLE (AP) - The Law School at the University of Memphis is expanding its academic offerings. In a press release made available earlier today, James Smoot, Dean of the Cecil C. Humphreys School of Law, announced the implementation of a new study program resulting in professional degree in Sharia Law, the prevalent legal framework found in Islamic cultures. In the statement, Dean Smoot noted that one of the primary missions of the state-funded Law School is to provide a superior and cutting-edge legal education to its students, enabling graduates to compete in emerging legal markets, as well as conventional methods of legal problem solving. According to the statement, the Law School administration and faculty has been researching the issue for several months and concluded it would be a mistake for the school to ignore the growing Muslim presence within the State of Tennessee, as well as the swelling population of illegal aliens, predisposed to embrace Muslim and Sharia traditions.

In conjunction with the new program, it was announced that Saif al-Din al-Fresco has been appointed Distinguished Professor of Law and Chair of the Sharia Law Department. Educated at Dar Al Uloom University in Riyadh, Saudi Arabia, al-Din al-Fresco served for four years as Solicitor General for Egyptian President Hosni Mubarak, and was Associate Justice of the Egyptian Supreme Council for almost nine years. In recent days he has served as adjunct faculty in Sharia Law and Islamic Studies at Sud-Est de Paris un Collège Communautaire, in Paris.

Response by public officials to the announcement has been mixed. Rep. Steve Cohen (D) of the 9th District was restrained but appeared troubled at a hastily scheduled press conference held on the front steps of the Law School. Rep. Cohen told the press in attendance that he was a 1976 graduate of the Memphis Laws School, and had long been active in fund raising activities for the school. Most recently Cohen and his staff has worked closely with the Law School, with GAO, and with the Post Office to facilitate the acquisition and renovation of the Old Custom House Building by the Law School, and the relocation of the campus from east Memphis to the downtown location, overlooking the Mississippi River. Although stopping short of criticizing the school, Rep. Cohen acknowledged that he would have preferred knowing about the decision making process in advance. "They have decided to place this new program right in the middle of my District, and I'm a Jew, for Christ's sake," said Cohen.

Reaction in Nashville on Capitol Hill was less restrained. Republican State Senator Bill Ketron declared the move by the Memphis Law School to be "outrageous." In February of this year, Ketron, along with Rep. Matheny of Tullahoma, introduced legislation in both state houses which would make it a felony to practice Sharia Law in Tennessee. Punishment for such acts would carry a punishment of up to 15 years imprisonment. Although the proposed legislation failed to gain traction in the 2011 session, Ketron has vowed to bring it back next year. Found at his modest home in Murfreesboro, Tennessee, Sen. Ketron said: "I assure you, the good people of Tennessee will not stand for this." In addition to reintroduction of the anti-Sharia legislation, Ketron also stated that he intends to look into State funding of the University of Memphis, suggesting that Tennessee may have "one state funded school too many."

The growing presence of Muslim culture and Sharia law has been a recurring event for Tennessee in recent months. In 2010, the construction of a proposed mosque within the city limits of Murfreesboro resulted in public demonstrations and lengthy litigation. Sen. Ketron, whose was outspoken in his opposition to the mosque in his hometown, filed his anti-Sharia bill at the beginning of the last legislative session, to great fanfare and debate. In early October of this year, the Hutton Hotel in downtown Nashville announced that it would cancel a Preserving Freedom Conference scheduled at the hotel for Veterans Day, November 11, which was slated to include some of the nation's leading opponents of Sharia Law, including Republican Representative Fred Grandy, who played the loveable character Gopher on the popular TV comedy Love Boat . A senior vice president for management said the hotel was not fully aware of the topic or the people involved when the event was booked, but now fears that the resulting protests could turn violent. He also said that some of the hotel's other guests had expressed concern.

Although an alternate location for the event has been located in nearby Madison, Tennessee, sponsors of the Preserving Freedom Conference remain embittered by the hotel's decision. Frank Gaffney, spokesman for the Sharia Awareness Action Network, said Monday that "this latest announcement by the Memphis Law School, coupled with the forced imposition of a Sharia-loving mosque on the good Christian people of Murfreesboro, and the unconstitutional and illegal actions of the Hutton Hotel in attempting to beat down the truth are all evidence that the state of Tennessee has been infiltrated by the Muslim Brotherhood, and now operates under Sharia Law."

Gaffney also points to undisclosed relationship of Tennessee's newly elected governor, Bill Haslam, to known Arab strongman, Abu Haslam.

The subject of Max Fleisher's 1937 scathing animated documentary, <u>Ali Baba's Forty Thieves</u>, Abu Haslam was renowned within the Arab community for his use of unrestrained violence and deceit in the plunder of nomadic settlements, during the first half of the 20th century.

Questions about the relationship between the governor and Abu Haslam arose during the 2010 campaign, which the candidate, and now governor steadfastly refused to answer. In previous inquiries, the governor's office has said that "Mr. Haslam's relations and his finances are nobody's business. We just don't see the public good in looking further into these prying question."

The governor's office had no response to Mr. Gaffney's A discussion of the forgoing news article is offered at LUNCH (DINNER) this Friday at the Gourmet Market and Casbah, in beautiful downtown Bearden. Dining will commence promptly at 11:49 o'clock AM, in accord with prevailing Sharia Law.

Wise Word 10

I have heard it suggested many times over that sports are so popular because they are a metaphor for life. Don't believe it for a minute. Sports finds the competitors embraced in a head-to-head battle, culminating with the declaration of a "victor" and, of course, the "loser."

I find most normal people are just trying to find respite from the noise...no desire to defeat someone, and certainly not anxious to subject themselves to the possibility of humiliation and defeat. This theory goes a long way toward explaining the veryt common phenomena of naps during televised games.

Nonetheless, I find myself swept up in the successes and failures of our local champions.
In recent days, we have seen the football team fall to the lowly and often mocked Big Blue, for the first time in something like 697 years, give or take. As a result, the football Vols are not even worthy of an invitation to one of 84 post season bowl games. Oh, the shame.

The basketball Vols have fared no better. Although perhaps clinging to the idea of a "moral victory" based on their performance in Hawaii against formidable opposition, they returned to the mainland this week, only to fall ignominiously to a mid-major team with the unlikely name of Oakland, looking awful in the effort. Oh, the shame.

The Lady Vols, whom we have come to depend upon as the stalwart of success in Big Orange Country, is now 4 and 3 for the season, after falling to the mighty Bible thumpers of Baylor, and their Goliath center. To make matters worse, the loss to Baylor represented the first home loss for the Lady Vols since 1922, or something like that.

My despair would be complete but for two serendipitous circumstances:
1. It appears that our coaching staff has not been fondling little boys; and
2. Ron Zook got fired. (I have been a faithful follower of the FireRonZook Webpage for many years).

No matter how far down the Big Orange program may fall, I take great pride in knowing we leave little boys alone, and we wouldn't hire Ron Zook for anything.

You will have an opportunity to share your favorite Ron Zook stories tomorrow at LUNCH (DINNER) at the Gourmet Market & Market at 11:50 o'clock AM.

You can expect to be joined by the long-lost and thawing Henry Naff, and perhaps a special guest appearance by the good Dr. Steve (Gimpy) Roberts, who has announced stretching his legs.

Wise Word 11

With the onset of the holiday season, and the year end fast approaching it seems appropriate to take a moment to look back and contemplate our circumstance. This LUNCH (DINNER) ensemble has been staggering along for 3 or 4 or 5 years now...it is hard to remember. During that time we have convened at no less than 5 separate eating establishments, at least two of which have gone out of business, caused in part, no doubt, by our patronage. We are a diverse group, with varied experiences and training, but upon reflection, I find we are still sadly lacking representation in one major field: Engineering.

We got 3 architects....but NO Engineers

We got no less than 4, (count 'em 4) lawyers....but not a single Engineer

We got government workers at the State, Local and Federal level.... but zero Engineers

We got an academician....but are without an Engineer

We got a PhD, for Pete's sake...but cannot find an Engineer

We got no less than two of societies rarest of creatures: professional musicians who actually make a comfortable living at their chosen profession... but not a dern-burn Engineer

We got a financial advisor....but no advise about where to find an Engineer

We got two published authors, one non-fiction, the other just lies.... but nary a single Engineer

We got a Rugby coach and a Foundation President...but grasp in the dark for an Engineer

We got guys that ride motorcycles and guys that wear cowboy boots (yeah, really....cowboy boots)....but not an Engineer in sight

We got Nanook of the North who mines diamonds in the frozen tundra...but we're frozen out of Engineers

We got at least 6 grandpappys, with another on the way...but have gone generations without an Engineer

We got two scout leaders including one with a Silver Beaver (make up your own comment here)....but can't rustle up an Engineer

We got gun nuts, and car nuts, and wing nuts, and maybe fruit cups... but nada an Engineer

We got guys who waste way too much time reading pointless email messages...but still no Engineer

But verily I say unto you, it looks as though there is a reasonable chance that this deficiency will be remedied. I cannot predict the exact odds of that chance, but believe that a competent Engineer could calculate it down to the 4th decimal place.

If the possibility comes to fruition, the impact will be enormous. Just recount the number of times one of us has offered: "Well, I know one thing for certain, they could fix the whole dang thing if they would just (here insert stupid idea)". Not only could an Engineer point out the folly of the suggestion with clarity, he should be able to quantify the magnitude of stupidity. I can't wait.

I do not proffer that Engineers are without flaws, for we all fall short. I am reminded of the testimony of our erstwhile teacher, David Walker, who confessed that during the course of his theological instruction, and after much prayerful consideration, he had come to the conclusion that God had relied upon the services of Engineers when designing the human body...since only an Engineer would situate a recreation area immediately adjacent to a waste treatment facility.

You may have your own insights on the value of Engineers, and you are invited to share them tomorrow at LUNCH (DINNER) commencing promptly at approximately 11:53 o'clock AM, at the Gourmet Market and Slide Rule Emporium, situate in beautiful downtown Bearden. Food services and child care will be available. In case of inclement weather, dress warmly.

Wise Word 12

This week I fully intended to present to you for your consideration a lengthy and detailed exposition on bovine mastitis, drawing largely from my Dad's undergraduate thesis, *circa* 1947. However, it now appears that I simply will not have adequate time for that project, since today is the Winter solstice... the shortest day of the year. We have oft been urged to "make hay while the sun shines." Unfortunately, today, there just isn't that much sunshine to work with.

You should anticipate that the solstice will arrive at 12:30 o'clock AM Eastern Standard Time, and I encourage you to prepare accordingly. With the knowledge that tonight will feature almost 9.8 hours of darkness, I have prepared by fluffing my pillow.

You should also mark your "To Do List" to note that the world will end one (1) year from today, in accord with the Mayan calendar. I have placed a call in to Harold Camping of Family Radio, who famously predicted the end of the world on both May 21 of this year and October 21. As you may be aware, his predictions have been largely debunked by much of the scientific community, and in fairness to the skeptics, Harold is O fer 2, so far. I intend to ask if he is now endorsing the Mayan deadline, and will let you know, as soon as he calls back.

In the meantime, the extra long evening hours should allow you to be sufficiently well rested to join LUNCH (DINNER) on Friday, the 3rd shortest day of the year, promptly at approximately 11:53 o'clock AM, at the Gourmet Market, located in beautiful, clement downtown Bearden. The weather forecast calls for cloudy conditions, with a high of 46 degrees and a 20% chance of rain. You are encouraged to dress both appropriately and demurely. If you are concerned about the wind chill factor, please use the newly revise North American Wind Chill Index formula:

where Chill is measured in Degrees of °F, and Wind is measured in mph.

Any questions regarding application of the formula should be directed to Kevin Anderson.

In planning activities for the remainder of the month, I note that 2012 is a Bissextile year, such that the horrid month of February has 29 days. The Santorum campaign has already announced its disgust with the circumstance and issued a campaign pledge to revoke the Georgian calendar.

By design, the Georgian calendar adds an extra day every four years to compensate for the fact that 365 days is slightly shorter than the solar year, by about, *but not exactly* , 6 hours. This designed formula, which results in the Bissextile years, also includes an exception , to wit: years that are evenly divisible by 100 are not Bissextile, unless that year is also evenly divisible by 400. So, in accord with the rule, and the exception, the average number of days per year is $365 + 1/4 - 1/100 + 1/400 = 365.2425 = 365$ days, 5 hours and 12 seconds. However, since the solar year is constantly increasing, the Georgian calendar is still going to off about one day every 8000 years or so...and on top of it all, my watch stopped working about two weeks ago.

The most important implication of the Bissextile year is that your Tennessee fishing license will have an additional full day of validity, not expiring until February 29th this year, rather than the much stingier February 28.

On the other hand you can take steps now to renew you license for next year at any time, at your convenience. I encourage you to do so, and am heartened by the testimony of Brother Penland who confesses to buying a license not with the intent of actually fishing, but only to support the activities funded by the modest fees collected at renewal.

In recent days I have strained to reach the conclusion that the call to fishing must be a direct mandate from God. Consider the following:
1. At least four (maybe more) of the Apostles were fishermen
2. Each of the Apostles were commissioned with "I will make you fishers (of men)"
3. They fed 5000 hungry, dirty faces with only two, count 'em two, fish
4. One time Simon Peter announced: "I am going out to fish," and all the others replied: "Hey,...we're going, too!"
5. According to John 21, after the crucifixion and resurrection, when Jesus went to catch up and say howdy to the disciples, they went fishing! And not only do we know that they went, but we know how many they caught...153 ...pretty impressive.
6. Early (First Century) Christians used the fish symbol, Ichthys, as a secret sign for those of kindred spirit. When meeting a stranger, the

early Christian would make a simple arc in the dirt. If the stranger completed the arc with another intersecting arc, then each knew the other to be a believer.

I've always thought that if Jesus knew his teachings had, in less than 100 years, devolved into secret symbols, he would be rolling over in his grave. I'm pretty sure, based on the foregoing, that Jesus was in favor of fishing, and fishing licenses, and I intend to be on his good side.

Perhaps more impertinent to this Bissextile year, however, is the compelling research of Edwin Haeberle and Rolf Gindorf, published originally in 1998. Based on the prior work on Demski and f Thresher, these research scientists have observed and reported on widespread Bissextile activity among various fish species, including the famed sea basses (*serranidea*), and even more shockingly, the reef dwelling wrasse (*thalasoma dupery*) which have been reported to have burst into flame during active social situations that feature disco balls and loud, pulsating music. Gratefully, I find no evidence of similar behavior being reported among the local trout population.

You are encouraged to investigate this startling matter further this Friday (day after tomorrow) at LUNCH (DINNER) at 11:51 o'clock AM at the Gourmet Market and Bait Shop, located in beautiful and swishy downtown Bearden. Free parking is available in the adjoining lot.

Wise Word 13

Having lived in Knoxville for close to half a century, I am always amazed by the number of people that live here that I do not know. I read the obituaries in the News-Sentinel every day, always assuming that I must know somebody in there, or at least some of the family members. That assumption is almost always an error. However, my devotion to the obituaries is not without fellow travelers. Last December, at a Christmas party I mentioned to a friend that I had seen a "Ford" from South Knoxville in the obituaries, who must have been an uncle or cousin of hers. Incidentally, there are Fords behind every stump in South Knoxville...have been for generations...hence East Ford Valley Rd; West Ford Valley Road; etc.

In the course of that conversation, another friend of approximately my age who has lived in the Knoxville only for a couple of years confessed that he, too, reads the obituaries daily. When asked why he would find Knoxville's obituaries interesting, he replied that he studies them for the over/under. Perhaps that 's really why I study them...

Irregardless, I find obituaries intriguing, particularly the variety of nicknames that pop up. Just in the last couple of weeks, I noted the following nicknames:
Pea; Granny; Derby; Chicken Man; Ace; Skinny; The Warden; Tut; Soulful; Papaw Bob; and my favorite: Rapture Ready Ruthi.

I still regret not having been ascribed a jaunty nickname in childhood, and must confess that my recent efforts to self-assign my nickname of "Mamaw" has not met with measurable success...go figure.

Some of you will recall a science teacher at old Young High School, Sam Kennedy, who was universally and affectionately known as "Moe". Gone for several years now, he was a long time member of Church Street, but as I recall, his obituary did not include his nickname. Some of you may also know or know his adult son from Church Street, who will be found at the back of the sanctuary pretty much every time the doors are unlocked. When I first met Jim in the early 1980's and told him that I was a South Knoxville survivor, he offered that his dad taught at Young, and recalled the nickname of Moe, but suggested he had no idea how the sobriquet could have originated. I held my tongue, and will leave it to you to reach your own conclusions.

To the south of the Shop Building and parking lot at Young High lay a deeply wooded ravine, into which no reasonable person would willingly wander. With the development on oversized earth-moving equipment, the ravine has long since been filled and now houses a Quickie Mart and a Mini Storage Warehouse, but at the time, it constituted unfettered suburban wilderness. At some point in the Spring of my sophomore year, Moe Kennedy approached the Key Club with a suggestion for a worthy service project, to wit: opening up a nature path through the wooded ravine, and naming the various trees situated along the path. As an underclassman and relatively new member of Key Club, I was not fully aware of the mission of the organization, and had not noticed any great enthusiasm for service projects from the wizened members. Nonetheless, several of the Seniors seemed to take a keen interest in the suggestion. Under the leadership of Phil Somebody, 8 or 9 guys got excused from 4th, 5th and 6th period classes to pursue the project. They first went to the Shop and secured several pieces of scrap wood, which Mr. Denton, our shell-shocked Shop teacher, sawed and milled into uniform size and shape. Mr. Denton also had a wood burning implement of some ilk, which he loaned to the guys, to engrave names into the wooden blanks, over the weekend.

The following Monday, the Key Club leaders proudly presented to Mr. Kennedy the results of their tree-naming efforts. The placards were skillfully carved, stained and shellacked to a glimmer.

The specific names I recall seeing carved out were: Agnes; Trudy; Conrad; Bernie; and, of course, Moe...There were many more, but for some reason the signs never got placed on the trees...an utter shame, I think.

You are encouraged to share your utter shame tomorrow at LUNCH (DINNER) at 11:52 AM o'clock, in the morning, at the "Gourm", in beautiful and woodsy downtown Bearden.

Wise Word 14

It is official...and duly confirmed by the Assistant Deputy Chief Meteorologist and Storm Tracker at WBIR and WBIR.com: Spring is HERE, as of two days ago, and none too soon, as far as I am concerned.

There is a plethora of variant definitions for the word "spring" in the English language, such as: to move rapidly or leap; to arise from a source; a coil; to make known suddenly; to get released from jail; a source or origin; a flow of water from the ground; resilient; (here insert additional examples). On the other hand, Spring, as a season of the Earth's annual cycle around the Sun, has no synonym.

Likewise the term "Fall" has multiple definitions: to come down by force of gravity; to become lower in amount; to be captured; to come into an inheritance; a cascade of water; a division of a wrestling match; a cheap hair extension; (here insert more dubious definitions). However, the definition for Fall, as describing one of the seasons, is blessed with the very functional and mellifluous synonym of Autumn....well that just ain't right

The term autumn is derived from the ancient Etruscan language, as passed through Old French dialect, and refers specifically to the autumnal equinox, occurring around September 22 of each year, (the beginning of Fall), when the Earth's axis tilts off-kilter from the Sun not one whit. Fortunately, there is second time each year when the Earth's axis is at a perfect right angle to the Sun, occurring around March 20, which, by wonderful serendipity, corresponds to the beginning of Spring. This point in our galactic life is known amongst the intelligentsia as the Vernal Equinox.

Since fair is fair, and right is right, if Fall gets the handy synonym of Autumn, then it is only reasonable that Spring should enjoy the equally useful synonym of Vern. I encourage you to substitute the term freely, particularly in musical context. I am drawn first to that old Rodgers and Hammerstein chestnut of 1945 from the classic Broadway play State Fair: "It Might As Well Be Vern". I also like the prospects of Mendelssohn's "Vern", and the Vern movement from Vivaldi's Four Seasons.

Your are invited to join Vern and me for LUNCH (DINNER) tomorrow at the Gourm, at 11:54 o'clock AM in beautiful downtown Bearden. Food will be served. Some may be absent due to Vern Break activities.

Wise Word 15

How often do we complain aloud, or mutter quietly to ourselves that our lives are too cluttered, our commitments too numerous, and our calendars too full? Well... there is no reason to stop now! And tomorrow is no exception.

In addition to the obligatory LUNCH (DINNER) meeting, please take note of the following matters for tomorrow's schedule:

1. National Doctor's Day – you are encourage to send a card, or, if appropriate, place flowers on your physician's grave
2. Frankie Laine's 99th birthday – celebrate by singing *Rawhide* in a public venue, including all the lyrics you never did really understand
3. The half-century mark for Stanley Kirk Burrell, known affectionately as MC Hammer – stand arrogantly on the sidewalk, challenge passers-by to "touch that", and then flout their failure with a mocking tone
4. For the 26th anniversary of James Cagney's death, commemorate breakfast by smashing a grapefruit into your wife's face (discretion advised)
5. Tola of Clonard Festival – free form celebration of your choosing, consistent with your personal beliefs. But, as always, no horseplay, and do not leave your Clonard in the hot sun for extended periods.

Please share the fruits of your celebrations tomorrow at LUNCH (DINNER) the Gourm. Mkt. & Rm., at exactly about 11:53 o'clock AM. Free Parking for those with the magic decal placed securely in the lower left quadrant of their windshield.

Wise Word 16

As many of you are aware, a few weeks ago Henry (Nanook) Naff lost his employment at a ketchup mining operation located somewhere deep inside the Arctic Circle (I may not have all of the details exactly correct, but the gist is there).

Henry has tied to put the best light on the matter, offering that the contract had simply expired at the expected time, and that he was looking forward to being in warmer climes, and hopefully being able to once again feel his toes, fingers and other extremity.

Well, Lady Fortune has again recast her gaze, and Henry has now been restationed to the lovely State of Oklahoma, where he is now engaged in monitoring and analyzing mule production. (Again, my details may be a little off, but you get the idea).

Although he has been in Oklahoma City only a few days, Henry has been getting more and more familiar with his new surroundings, and offers the following observations about the Sooner State:

1. The wind comes sweeping down the plain
2. The waving wheat can sure smell sweet
3. The wind comes right behind the rain
4. There is an opportunity every night to sit alone watching a hawk making lazy circles in the sky
5. The land is grand; and
6. "Yeeow! Ayipioeeay!" in Oklahoma-speak is the equivalent of saying "You're doing fine, Oklahoma!"

In order to celebrate this fine and unexpected turn of events, you are invited to SUPPER (DINNER) on Saturday, May 26, 2012, at the Steve and Linda Wise cabin, situate in the bucolic Fountain City Sportsmen's Club, on beautiful Norris Lake. We will eat at 6:30 o'clock PM EDST, or thereabouts, but you are invited to come on up about 2:00 o'clock PM EDST, or so, for boat rides, conversation, conviviality, beverage depletion, and the like. Also, and perhaps most importantly, spouses, paramours and significant others are also invited to the event, so you won't have to ask for permission.

Since the Gourmet Brothers, Ulysses, Cosmo and Al, will not be around to provide the victuals, I will need to get a nose count to prepare appropriately, so let me know if you can make it.

I will send a map in a following email, as soon as I can get it fixed....the trip takes about 35 minutes from downtown...less if you drive like my brother.

Wise Word 17

UT Baseball is now sadly closed for the season, but the ballgames have just begun. One of the enduring attractions of America's pastime is the endless statistics and trivia . For instance, the first jersey to be retired was ole Number 4 of Lou Gehrig in 1939. The only number to be permanently from all of baseball is Jackie Robinson's 42.

To challenge you synapses, I offer the following trivia question: During the modern era (our lifetime) the Cincinnati Reds changed their name temporarily. As a two part bonus question, What name did they change to, and why?

In order to increase the interest, the person with the first correct answer by reply email will win a $100.00 Gift Certificate to The Regas Restaurant, Knoxville's Gathering Place.

The winner will be announced, and the award ceremony will be held tomorrow at LUNCH (DINNER) at 11:49 o'clock AM, at the Gourmet Market and Cosmos, in beautiful downtown Bearden

(Prize awards are subject to tax, title, dealer prep and undercoating fees; the decision of the judges is final; offer not valid in MN, ARK, NV, MS, Portland, Neb, VT, TN, Calif, Boise, Seville, Ballparks, Wash, Local restaurants, Bearden and Vegetable gardens; promotional sponsor is not related to Burlington Coat Factory; side effects may include runny nose, diarrhea, constipation, drooling, stiffness of joints; facial twitching; splayed feet, coughing like an asthmatic monkey, lingering attraction to show tunes, earwax build-up, and incontinence. If stiffness of joints continues for more than 4 hours, consult a physician; offer and prize awards have no cash value; Subject to the terms and provisions of 12 CFR 14.2284B(55.09), Subsection 229944.99474, Article J)

Wise Word 18

As a younger man, I rarely if ever pondered the complexities of ambiguity, most likely due to self-doubt , and the assumption that the rest of the world understood nuances better than I did.

Now, in my more pensive years, I find that uncertainty of meaning, or uncertainty of application, or uncertainty of intent arising from ambiguity can be troubling ...or thrilling...or intriguing. It just depends.

Instances of moral ambiguity are always the most difficult, and usually the most troubling. I try to avoid them. Other types of ambiguity cause less stress and *can* be a welcome diversion. It just depends

Last Friday, as I was lingering over my repast, I chose to listen idly to the conversation of others. At one point, for some unknown reason, Jim Rogers asked of Bill Reeves whether he wore boxers or briefs, to which Bill Replied: "" Depends..."

You will have an opportunity to resolve this ambiguity by further inquiry this Friday, at LUNCH (DINNER) at 11:53 o'clock AM, at the Gourmet Market and Geriatric Center, in beauteous around town Bearden Village District.

As a special bonus, Dave Collins, using his far-reaching political contacts, has persuaded his friend, County Commissioner Jeff Ownby, to join us this Friday to provide a short audio-visual presentation.

The topic will be: *The Expectations of Privacy for Local Elected Officials in Public Parks.*

You don't want to miss it.

Wise Word 19

Tomorrow, 11:56 o'clock AM; Cosmo's Grill at the Gourmet Market, in beautiful downtown Beardsley. Food and beverage will be served for a modest price.

I will, sadly, not be able join the assemblage, as I will be on my way to see the Yankees versus the Nats at beautiful and inviting Nationals Park located in Southeast Washington, south of the Capitol, along the fast-developing Capitol Riverfront adjacent to the Navy Yard. The new park not only redefines modern sports facility architecture but also serves as the catalyst and cornerstone of a new mixed-use Capitol Riverfront in our nation's capital. Also, there's an engagement party thingy, too.

Stories of redemption and recovery from a fall from grace are always heartwarming, and often provide us with valuable life lessons which we can take and judicially apply to our own lives. America has been blessed with such a story in recent days, and we should celebrate and embrace the telling. Just last week, one of the most despised and reviled men of our generation was fully redeemed and returned to the graces of society when LeBron James, in the accompaniment of his Miami Heat teammates, plowed his way to the NBA Championship in five games, over the Oklahoma City Thunder. (Who knew Oklahoma City even had a basketball team).

In honor of this extraordinary turn of events, it seems only just that the win-a-prize trivia question this week should come from the world of professional basketball. This idea is further reinforced by your prompt and seemingly effortless answers the prior baseball trivia questions. I note with interest Rick Armbrister's comment that "anyone with half an internet" could divine the correct response, and have concluded that the internet is a vast baseball trivia conspiracy, designed to frustrate my efforts.

In any event, here you go. Before Kobe Bryant, before Michael Jordan, before even Michael Jackson, for that matter, America got to enjoy the massive talents of The Big E—Elgin Baylor.

After a stellar career at Springham High School in Washington, DC, Baylor sought after by a variety of collegiate programs. Due to some academic shortcomings, his career was short-tracked until he signed a football and basketball scholarship at the College of Idaho, in beautiful downtown

Caldwell, Idaho.

After one season, the College fired the basketball coach and pretty much shut down the program, leaving young Elg high and dry. After spending a year on an AAU team located in the Great Northwest, our hero signed to play at Seattle University, a Jesuit school located, not surprisingly, in Seattle. It was during his tenure at The Emerald City that breadth of The Big E's talents began to unfold. In his senior year of 1958, Elg led the Seattle Chieftains to the NCAA national championship game against perennial contenders , the Kentucky Wildcats, under the leadership of Adolf Rupp.

This reminds me of a *Sports Illustrated* article of a few years ago reporting on the recruitment of eventual Kentucky quarterback, Tim Couch. The article reported that the Wildcat coaches were so dedicated to signing him that for months they "stayed on top of him like...well...a cat on a couch."

Anyway, in spite of a magnificent effort by Baylor in the championship game, including 25 points and 19 rebounds, the mighty Chieftains fell to Kentucky 84 to 72.

Elg was the number 1 draft choice in 1958 NBA draft, selected by the Minneapolis Lakers in the first round, taken ahead of such luminaries as Bennie Swain and Joe Quigg.

In the NBA, The Big E earned Rookie of the Year honors in 1959, and was an 11 time NBA All-Star. He was inducted into the Naismith Hall of Fame, and after his playing days eventually became GM of the Los Angeles Clippers.

In one particularly stellar performance in the 1962 NBA Championship series, Elg scored an amazing 63 points against the Boston Celtics . In a post game locker room interview, when asked about the pivotal element of the game, one of Baylor's teammates famously explained: "Elg and me went for 65 tonight." Who is that player?

In order to sweeten the pot, and in recognition of pending holiday celebration, the prize for the first correct answer will no longer be merely a gift certificate to a local restaurant, No, no, no...this week's winner will be awarded :

TWO FREE PASSES to the LEE GREENWOOD THEATRE located along the shore of beautiful Douglas Lake in bucolic Sevierville Tennessee. In addition to a fine dining experience, featuring fried chicken, mashed potatoes, corn bread, and some brown stuff , you will be entertained by the dulcet tones of that fine All American crooner, Lee Greenwood , including a medley of his greatest hit, *Proud to Be an American* (where at least I know I'm free), as well as a shorter, but still insufferable medley of his lesser hit, *Proud to Be an Canadian (where at least I know I'm free)*.

As an added bonus, our own Dave Collins has promised to use his influence and call in his political chips to insure that you will be accompanied on your dining and entertainment adventure with local celebrity, birdwatcher, nature lover, and bon vivant, Commissioner Jeff Ownby. So enter early and often.

The winner will be announced this Friday at LUNCH (DINNER) at the Gourmet Market and Cosmos, at 11:53 o'clock AM. Don't be early. Taxes, title and undercoating still apply. You must be present to win. Must be 21 months old to enter. Decision of the judges is final. Do not squint. Keep your mouth closed when chewing.

Wise Word 20

I continue to be distressed by the apparent ease with which the sports trivia questions are answered, particularly in light of the intelligence level of the participants. I thought that shifting from baseball trivia to the more arcane basketball trivia would slow down the response time, but noooooo. The widespread availability of free internet search engines coupled with even a modicum of typing skills apparently can turn anyone into Alex Trebek. Accordingly, I must shift venues once again, if only to give my internet server a rest.

This week's issue of *Sports Illustrated* contains a "where are they now?" article featuring one of my favorite running backs of all times, Earl Campbell. After a stellar career at the *other* UT, including winning the Heisman Trophy in 1977, Campbell was the number one draft pick of the NFL, being selected by the Houston Oilers (now Tennessee Titians).

As an Oiler, Campbell was a punishing running back in the mold of Jim Brown, that knocked defenders sideways and drug them down the field. When Earl first signed with Texas, he came to campus with the intention of being a defensive end, because he liked punishing opponents. The coaching staff made him watch films of Jim Brown to show that a good running back has the same opportunity to hurt people as defensive players, and he agreed to the shift.

As an example of his approach to the game, the article remembers an incident early in Campbell's career at Texas, when he took the ball hard through the line to the corner of the end zone where he plowed into Bevo, the schools 1,700 pounds pet Longhorn.

Earl recalls, "I hit him in the flank, right here," ..., pointing at the midsection of a longhorn sculpture that happened to be on hand. "Bevo took most of the blow. He didn't fall, but I could feel him stumble backward. After he got his balance, he looked at me and said, 'Moo.'"

Whether out of superstition or just habit, Campbell followed a tradition beginning in high school in Tyler, Texas, and continuing throughout his collegiate and professional career. While dressing, Earl would always place something in his left shoe. What is it?

The first correct answer receives three (3) free passes to Porpoise

Island in the Smokeys, formerly located in beautiful downtown Pigeon Forge, along with one (1) free pass to the famed Bonnie Lou and Buster Show Theatre, formerly just down the street. Enter early and often. The lucky winner will be announced tomorrow at LUNCH (DINNER) at Cosmos Grill, at 11:55 o'clock AM. All the prior qualifying conditions apply, so don't mess with me.

Wise Word 21

The obituaries of the Knoxville News-Sentinel continue to intrigue and baffle me. This week's paper makes note of the passing of an 82-year-old Loudon businessman, who served his country in the Armed Forces, remained married to the same woman for almost half a century, successfully raised four (4) daughters to adulthood and independence, and was apparently well liked, if not beloved, in his community. Nonetheless, his obituary asserts that he "was best known for his dip dogs." I don't know what to think.

In my professional capacity I have very recently been called upon to consult with the Indonesian National Badminton Team with regard to an emerging dispute with the World Badminton Federation. I do not yet have details of the problem, but find that the demands of that project will preclude me from preparing and forwarding a reminder memo today about LUNCH (DINNER) tomorrow at 11:51 o'clock AM at the Gourmet Market and Cosmos, in beautiful downtown Beardsome.

In such circumstances, Article 14 b, Section 19.335946, paragraph 3a664g of our Bylaws, provides that the memo preparation task falls to the duly elected Chairman of the Committee on Communications and Emails, Grainger (County Tomato) Morrison.
Accordingly, you should expect a reminder memo directly from County Tomato by 1:30 today. If, for any reason, you fail to receive your reminder timely, please do not hesitate to contact Grainger with your complaints, at your convenience.

The migration of humankind and all of God's creatures in search of sustenance and bounty is a common and recurrent theme coursing throughout history, providing us with tales of marvel, and wonder, and despair.

The story of the movement of the Jews across the desert for 40 years during the Exodus, surviving on manna, and in search of the land of milk and honey is indelibly etched into the mind of every child of Western Civilization.

In more modern times, the most powerful nation in the world was rocked and battered by the western migration of families from the Great Plains during the Dust Bowl era, all in search of sustenance and opportunity in the land of plenty.
And who among us cannot remember with sympathy the plight of the lowly

boll weevil, who rose up from the crippling poverty of Mexico, and traveled for miles and miles in a series of teeny tiny steps all the way to Texas, justa looking for a home, Lord, Lord, justa looking for a home.

Curiously, our lowly, peripatetic ensemble now finds itself in the same circumstance...on a lonely, seemingly endless voyage in search of a suitable place to eat.
Based on the overwhelming response to last week's dining choice, we are moving on yet again. PAY ATTENTION.

This week, LUNCH (DINNER) will be enjoyed ay Jason's Deli, located at the corner of Cumberland and 22nd Street, across the side street from the recently demolished OCI and the recently demolished, world famous Tap Room.
There is plenty of free parking to the rear off the building, and the most recent Health Department rating is well within acceptable standards.
Per usual, we will convene at 11:51 o'clock AM, with a unison recitation of the Apollo Creed. Don't be late.

Wise Word 22

Homecoming is a time of remembrance, of reuniting and relaxation, and of respite, and this week has shown itself to be a bit of a Homecoming period for much of our ensemble.

Brother Woodson has, at long last returned home from his visit at Fort Sanders Hospital, courtesy of the Bill Penland courier and delivery service. Bob is reported (and is reporting) to being resting comfortably, and healing up nicely. We fully expect a complete report from Bill including all the appropriate details. If none is forthcoming, we shall, of course, revert to the standard practice of making up our own stories about the cause and disposition of the hospital stay. Grainger has already posited that it is the unfortunate result of a Pap smear gone horribly bad, but we can wait for details.

Henry has returned home from the northern climes, and is reported to be thawing nicely.

Jim Rogers has finally gotten back home after trying fruitlessly to sell parking spaces for the UT – Akron game in the parking lot of Church of the Good Shepherd in Fountain City (some habits die hard).

Bill Reeves and Edward Peterson are both back home from Family Weekend at Rhodes College in Memphis, after enjoying all of the thoughtfully planned family activities on campus, and the Bursar's friendly reminder that next Semester's tuition will be due in just a few short days.

Our own good Dr. Steve is back home again from his lovely sojourn to Mobile , Alabama...a city whose latest marketing brand is: "Really not all that far from Biloxi!"

And Brother Butch is thankfully back home at last from that cold, dark, scary place located deep in the furthermost recesses of his mind...so distant that only *he* can safely visit there and return.

To all I say: "Welcome Home!"

In addition to his standard duties of being aware of all fire events in the City of Knoxville, but attending to none, Brother John Rodgers has, for the last several months, taken roll and maintained attendance records at our weekly gatherings, as part of a data gathering program instituted by Chairman LaFevor. This past week John reported that 47% of our brood have been enjoying and benefitting from the weekly reminder memos, but have failed to attend the LUNCH (DINNER) gatherings with measurable regularity. Based upon that surprising data, Ken Wise has prepared a White Paper report for the Chairman, which concludes that "pert near one-half of our ensemble sees themselves as victims; think that the rest of the LUNCH (DINNER) group must carry their load; do not take care of their personal responsibilities; or even care for their lives." Do I hear an "AMEN" from the righteous 53%?

I am certainly not one to judge, nor one to offer unsolicited advice... but...

DON'T be a leech on society...join LUNCH (DINNER) tomorrow at Jason's Deli, promptly at 11:53 o'clock AM, in beautiful Fort Sanders, where the slovenly 43% come to frolic.

Wise Word 23

If you have been paying attention even the slightest bit in the last few months, you are aware that we are in the throes of a hotly contested Presidential election campaign, pitting an established incumbent of dubious talents against un upstart pretender of equally dubious talents.

Remarkably, and in spite of the plethora of campaign messages, attack ads, and pundit head spinning there still exists a disturbing bloc of undecided voters, or, as they are more commonly referred to: stupid people who should not be entitled to vote.

So, as a public service to those remaining citizens who have yet to see the puck, we are sponsoring a town hall format Presidential debate tomorrow at Jason's Deli on the infamous Strip in the historic Fort Sanders community, beginning promptly at 11:51 o'clock AM.

Incumbent President-for-Life, Jim Lafevor, with his infernal cry of "Forty More Years!" will lock horns with his upstart challenger, Kevin Anderson, who is sure to pose the question: "Are your LUNCHes (DINNERs) better today than they were four years ago?"

Although parking in the rear is , as always, plentiful, it is expected that seating will be scarce, so come early, and vote often. Food will be made available at a modest cost.

Wise Word 24

When we first moved into our place on Mountaincrest, about 14 years ago, there were five (5) (V) thriving Bradford Pear trees, all clumped together in the side yard, next to the main driveway. With the passage of time, coupled with my benign neglect, all but one of those Bradford pears has splintered, collapsed, and been hauled away in bit size pieces. The wood is so ridiculously soft, that I have managed, on more than one occasion, to cut up an entire 25 foot tree with nothing more than a bow saw.

One hardy example remains, and I have taken up the mission to insure its survival, by having it professionally "lolly-popped" very few years, which is nothing more than cutting the foliage back to make it look like a deformed telephone pole. Surprisingly, within a season, the growth returns, and it once again looks like a child's drawing of a tree.

The primary reason that I have gone to the trouble to protect this plant is because it serves as my seasonal harbinger. Although that tree is the very last to loose its leaves, never falling until mid-December, it is also the first to note the coming of Spring, and I am proud to announce that Wednesday morning, the first buds of Spring have arisen on my singular Bradford Pear!

The days are getting longer (for now the last 20 days), and with the Bradford Pear having asserted itself, I am hereby declaring Winter as officially OVER.... OVER, I say. I even saw the second most important harbinger on the way home last night: a billboard advertising the Boat Show. Put on your short pants, cowboy!

In order to celebrate, you are encourage to join for LUNCH (DINNER) tomorrow at Jason's Deli at 11:48 o'clock AM, in beautiful downtown Cumberland Avenue Corridor. Season vittles will be made available.

Wise Word 25

I am not one that is normally plagued by self doubt. If fact, absolute confidence, without regard to any inconvenient countervailing facts, sentiment, or argument is a basic hallmark of my profession and livelihood. That circumstance probably accounts, at least partially, for the level of community respect enjoyed by members of the Bar.
Nonetheless, I am beginning to question my earlier declaration last week that winter is, at last over...OVER, I say.

The basic premise remains true: winter solstice has passed; the days are getting longer; the Bradford Pear tree holds new buds aloft. But for some nagging reason, I am beginning to question the truth of the declaration.

Accordingly, we shall entertain a full unbridled debate of the matter tomorrow at LUNCH (DINNER) at Jason's Deli, located in the heart of the edge of downtown, feature free and convenient parking.

Come prepared to defend your position, with semi-automatic weaponry, if deemed appropriate.

Wise Word 26

I don't normally shop. I don't enjoy it, and the facts are that I am just not very good at it. My attention span is short, and my patience with other shoppers and shopkeepers is shorter. If I need a pair of pants, just about anything will do, so long as it has two leg openings, does not chafe or bind, and stops above the bottom of my shoes.

Stores themselves present a strange dichotomy. Fountain City got a "Super" Kroger a couple of years ago. I am both fascinated and repelled by it. Stepping inside you are overwhelmed by the size, and possibilities, but actually trying to find the Oreos and beef jerky that you so desperately need is frustrating beyond tolerance.

As a result, I have reach a happy accommodation with my spouse regarding grocery shopping: She does it. In those infrequent instances when the shopping burden shifts to me, I always take my phone with me, call Linda upon entering the store, read the food item needed, and she directs me to the appropriate aisle location. Although simple and efficient, the systems is not foolproof.

Recently I found myself tasked with buying toothpaste, Crest Toothpaste, specifically...a seemingly simple responsibility. However, after locating the toothpaste aisle (one row east from headache medicine and Depends), I was confronted with intelligently choosing from among the following Crest options:

Pro Health Whiting
Whitening with Scope
Multi Benefit
Complete
Dual Blast Scope
Whitening
Cavity Protection
Tartar Protection
Baking Soda and Peroxide
Sensitivity
Vivid 3 D White
Deep Clean Effect
Extra White Scope
Extra White and Tartar Protection

Glamorous White Enamel Renewal

Complete Extra White Scope Effect; and, of course , that old favorite, Clinical Plaque Control

Like so many brainwashed participants in our consumer driven economy, I want EVERYTHING, and I want it NOW!

I want whitening, I want Scope, I want cavity protection, I want tartar protection, I want reasonable sensitivity to my needs, I want deep cleaning, I want extra whiteness, I want renewed enamel, and, yes, admitting the shame of it all, I want clinical plaque control...I WANT IT ALL!!

People have been worrying over the cleanliness of their teeth since before recorded history. The first records of dental hygiene date from 1600 BC, with the advent of the Ming Chow Chewing Stick. The Chinese dominated the international market, at least as to innovation, by introduction of the bristle brush in the 600's AD, featuring a variety of attractive bristle options, ranging from hog hair to horse tail hair.

As China forged ahead in dental technology, Western Civilization lagged far behind, relying on rubbing teeth with a nasty old rag covered with soot and salt, until the 1780s, when the first mass produced toothbrush was at last introduced, featuring the long beloved badger hair. By 1795, the State of Alabama had already adopted the time honored family tradition of the hand-me-down toothbrush.

The earliest record of a deliberate dentifrice formula came from the ancient Greeks who offered a concoction of crushed oyster shells (rubbed on with a dirty old rag, I suppose). By the 1800s Americans could buy tooth powder to go with their fancy new badger hair brushes, made up of pulverized charcoal, burnt bread, burnt alum and cinnamon. Yum, yum.

Toothpaste has been with us since late in the 19th century, but the variations and options seemed to have proliferated in just my lifetime.

Chuck Norris may have been the worst television actor since Wally Cox, who was abysmal, except, of course for his stellar voice over work as *Underdog.*

> *When in this world the headlines read*
> *Of those whose hearts are filled with greed;*
> *Who rob and steal from those in need;*

To right these wrongs with blinding speed goes:
UNDERDOG, underdog,
UNDERDOG. underdog.
Speed of lightening, Roar of thunder,
Fighting those who rob or plunder,
Underdog, ooh, ooh , ooh, ooh, ooh,
UNDERDOG, underdog.

In fairness, I can't say that I ever watched *Walker, Texas Ranger.* But I did see several promotional teasers and previews that always featured Chuck clumsily slobbering out an unveiled threat to some miscreant, followed by what has been described as a "Round House Kick", to punctuate the threat . Even if the "acting" had not been so bad, I probably could not have gotten past Chuck's porn star mustache or the creepy $13.75 toupee.

Perhaps because of the stupidity of the program, or the cartoon-like persona of *Walker, Texas Ranger,* the interweb has produced a huge collection of "Chuck Norris Facts" that serve to refine, define and solidify the true legacy of *Chuck Norris - Real life Action Figure.* Some of my favorites include:

- Chuck Norris can cut through a knife with hot butter.
- Chuck Norris can divide by zero.
- When he goes to bed at night, Superman wears Chuck Norris pajamas.
- Chuck Norris punched Cyclops between the eyes.
- Chuck Norris doesn't wear a watch...he decides what time it is.
- What was going through the minds of all of Chuck Norris' victims before they died? Chuck Norris' shoe, from a Round House Kick to the head.
- Chuck Norris took a horse to water...and then made it drink
- Nocturnal animals simply cannot sleep knowing that Chuck Norris is lurking about
- The only word in the English language that rhymes with orange is Chuck Norris
- Objects in Chuck Norris' mirror are closer to death than they appear.
- Chuck Norris built Rome in a day

I probably would never have thought of Chuck Norris again (thankfully) except for the intrepid work of Fox News, which apparently had a recent segment entitled:
" *Are Any Chuck Norris Facts True?*" I simply do not know what to make of it...I feel

like we have all taken a Round House Kick to the head. But, I will welcome your thoughts and explanations tomorrow at LUNCH (DINNER) at Jason's Deli at 11:51 o'clock AM on beautiful Cumberland Avenue. Foodstuff (and a Round House kick to the head) will be available.

Wise Word 36

As we have discussed in the past, I am a regular peruser of the obituaries in the local newspaper. Generally, I look for those that I know. However, as I have moved into the 6th decade on this orb, I am also regularly scanning for the over/under, and the odds continue to deteriorate.

I note there was a fine obituary earlier this week for Bubba Butts of Sevier County. I did not know Bubba Butts, which is a matter I find distressing, as I am confident that anyone named Bubba Butts must have interesting stories to tell.

Recently I have taken up reviewing the Birth Announcements, found in the Living Section of the Sunday News Sentinel (an altogether appropriate section to locate such announcements). My primary impetus for the review is to see how often new parents are inclined to name their offspring "Steve" or even "Stephen"...two of my favorite names. The results are troubling.

In the last few weeks, I have not found a single instance of a newborn at a Knox County Hospital being named Steve! There has been a Ca'Marah, a Maximus Quimby, a Jair and even a Zylus, but not a single Steve.

There has been two (2) Sinceres, one (1) Tashae Can'trice and a Ronoray, but yet no Steve. There has even been a Yullaina, a Kiss, and even a Madness (who in their right mind would chose to name a baby Madness?), but still no Steve. I am nonplussed, and flummoxed..

Before now I have always considered "Steve" to be a perfectly acceptable name. My confidence is shaken. On the other hand, my friend, the good Dr. Roberts, says that he shares my estimation on the value of that name...and he is an educated man.

Your views and opinions on name values will be solicited and entertained tomorrow at LUNCH (DINNER) at Jason's Deli on Cumberland Avenue, at approximately 11:50 o'clock AM. Be prepared to defend your position.

Wise Word 37

Well...I have continued to monitor the birth announcements, and I remain distressed. This week there was a Ju'Kiah, a Ma'Lejah, an E'Siya and a X'Zarius, but still no Stephen, or even a S'Tephen...go figure...

I thought perhaps the name had become laden with some less than attractive quality that served to remove it from the baby naming marketplace, like "Adolph" for instance. But that does not appear to be the case.

Admittedly, the Biblical Stephen carries with it the unsavory tradition of being stoned to death, On the other hand,, in an historical context, his stoning turned out to be a somewhat positive event for his legacy as the first Christian martyr.

Derived from the Greek (as reflected in a series of unintelligible squiggly lines), the name Stephen means "garland" or "crown".... not too shabby. I have been unable discern the meaning or the history of X'Zarius.

I had always assumed that the name "Steve" was merely a diminutive of Stephen, but that is not necessarily the case. From the ancient Romani, the name is held to mean: "Lummox sitting in the corner with drool on his cassock". All in life is not necessarily pretty.

I have learned that names are a funny thing. Just ask Grainger about his first name...hysterical.

Brother Ken is actually a Jr., a fact I either didn't know or make consequence of until my teenage years. Everybody called him by his middle name Ken, or the diminutive Kenny, until his college roommates, the Phillips brothers insisted on referring to him exclusive as "Norman". It is a tradition that, sadly, did not survive the college years. In fairness, the Phillips brothers were known among all their peers as "Crash" and "Doobie".... almost certainly not the names their mother vested upon them at birth.

Names will be drawn from a hat tomorrow at LUNCH (DINNER) at J'Ason's Deli on Cum'Berland Avenue at 11:53 o'clock AM...be there, or your good name will be besmirched.

Wise Word 38

I am a bit tardy in reminding you of your pending LUNCH (DINNER) obligations, inasmuch as I have been attending to Linda this afternoon for her LASIK surgery with the inimitable Dr. Harris. Since she only had her right eye attended to, I suppose it could be argued that she only has received LASIK/2 surgery.

All went well and she is now enjoying a Valium induced nap on the couch. I wish I slept that well...

This is my second encounter with LASIK surgery: initially as a patient, where the view was markedly impaired; and now, as a doting spouse, sitting at the foot of the patient, where the view and the total experience was much more enlightening and exciting.

If you have not had such surgery from David, I strongly urge you to consider it, even if your eyesight is perfect. Watching him do what he does is just plain astounding...

Today David was shadowed by a young doctor or med student (I am not sure which, as either I wasn't listening, or David mumbled during the introduction). During the second portion of the procedure which involves teeny-tiny work by hand, the shadow doctor/student watched with his mouth agape and head nodding in amazement. I have noticed that I don't have that same effect on other lawyers...go figure...

The only negative of the whole event is that due to the effects of 10 mg of Valium on my spouse, I must fend for myself for supper. Based on prior experiences in similar circumstances, I suspect that I will be mightily hungry by tomorrow at LUNCH (DINNER) at Jason's Deli at approximately 11:49 o'clock AM. You are encourage to watch me dine.

Wise Word 39

The Management Committee and Secretariat of our LUNCH (DINNER) ensemble gathered earlier this week, and after:

Prayerful consideration,
Thoughtful deliberation,
Open, honest discussion,
A healthy exchange of views,
An aggressive review of the implications.
A tenacious debate,
Some elevated voices,
A handful of poorly chosen words,
Some angry rebuttals,
Harsh confrontations,
Veiled threats,
Vigorous shaking of the fist,
The bearing of teeth,
Angry shouted warnings,
An unexpected bitch slap,
The unnecessary destruction of tables and chairs
Two episodes of fisticuffs,
Four bloodied noses,
The brandishing of weapons,
A brief but bloody knife fight,
A splenetic display of a hand gun,
Shots fired,
A noisome shootout,
A frenetic call to 911, and
A creepy kissing and making-up session,

determined that Friday will not occur at all this week, such that LUNCH (DINNER) will next convene on Friday, April 25, at 11:53 o'clock AM, at Jason's Deli.
Happy Easter to all, and be thankful for the deliberative process of an orderly society

Wise Word 40

Since last week had only 6 (six) (VI) days, *and* due to the commencement of Durwood Arts Festival festivities, *and* in recognition International Malaria Awareness Day, the managing cabal of the LUNCH (DINNER) ensemble has determined that LUNCH (DINNER) will convene tomorrow, Friday, April 25, at 11:49 o'clock AM at Jason's Deli on teeming Cumberland Avenue.

Do not resist the cabal.

Wise Word 41

I acknowledge that the weekly LUNCH (DINNER) reminder memos have been a bit of hit and miss over the last few weeks. I attribute the problem partly to my misapprehension that Lois Hammett have volunteered to assume the task. I know now that my conclusions in that regard were misguided and foolish at best.

I also attribute a portion of the problem to the fact that I have been covered up at work...but the truth is that the primary cause is a roaring case of writers' block. When I pointed my problem out to the good Dr. Roberts earlier this week, he opined that in light of the historical quality of my missives, my malady might better be described as writer's constipation.

I generally try to be receptive to constructive criticism, but his observation seems a bit harsh.

My confusion regarding Lois Hammett was, of course, driven by her email announcement that after 4 long years of service, she was withdrawing from the task of preparing and publishing the weekly news memo for the Parables Sunny School Class. At the time my conclusions made perfect sense... she had played in the minor league, and was ready to move up to the bigs.

Irregardless, the withdrawal of Lois has created a potentially volatile situation for our community, in that the Parables' newsletter mantle has been taken up by none other than our own Grainger Morrison, and his lovely bride, Paula. Be assured that I have unflagging confidence in Paula,...but Grainger!??! ...not so much.

Many of you will recall that the LUNCH (DINNER) Communications Committee appointed Grainger to supply the LUNCH (DINNER) reminder memo on a short term interim basis a couple of years ago, and we were all confronted with an extremely vivid photograph of Grainger's underpants, filled with rodents. I shutter now at the memory.

Our Lunch (DINNER) is composed of stout, toughened and burly men, and the repercussions of Grainger's memo were survived, even though the image is forever burned in our memories. The makeup of the Parables Sunny School Class is entirely different. Imagine the disaster if some of the more "delicate" class members were occasioned to stare into the abyss of

Grainger's underpants. Precautions must be take.

The matter will be discussed tomorrow at LUNCH (DINNER) at Jason's Deli at 11:47 o'clock AM.

Victuals will be served.

Wise Word 42

Thrice now I have arranged for a mechanic to travel up to Union County to repair the engine on my 15-year-old boat. On the initial two visits, the problem was gently diagnosed as "Operator Error."

As of yesterday, on the most recent visit, the mechanics actually found something wrong. I don't whether to be relieved, perplexed, embarrassed or disgusted.

Your input and consolation will be solicited tomorrow at LUNCH (DINNER) at Jason's Deli on bizzy Cumberland Avenue, beginning promptly at 11:41 o'clock AM. Free parking in the rear...

The word on the street is that for the first time in many weeks, we will be joined by the Good Right Rev. Dr. Roberts, walking upright and with a near normal gait!

Wise Word 43

LUNCH (DINNER) last week was remarkable in that we were blessed by the triumphant return of one of the institution's founders/charter members, the Good Dr. Roberts, proudly displaying his near normal simian-like gait, all due to the miracle of modern medicine.

The likelihood of his return this week cannot yet be assessed due to lack of reliable data, but hope remains alive. We can report that there exists a reasonable possibility that we will, this week, enjoy the company of jungle explorer, Prof. Naff, and his discussion of skin lesions and rashes prevailing in the subtropical Americas.

You will not want to miss that appetizing presentation, which commences TOMORROW, Friday, July 25, 2014, at 11:46 o'clock AM in the Jungle Lounge of Jason's Deli. Don't be late, and someone please give me a functioning email address for Penland...otherwise I fear he will not be properly fed and watered.

Wise Word 44

In what is believed to be a first for our LUNCH (DINNER) gathering, last week we were joined by a distaff member of our species, to wit: Gervis' lovely wife, Paula Morrison. All were glad to see her and made her feel welcome, but it was readily apparent that her presence altered the atmosphere around the table.

Discussion topics were a bit more tempered; opinions and observations were expressed with sightly less vigor; and, Mr. Armbrister and Mr. Woodson were both observed eating with utensils and napkins, rather than just their fists, as one would normally expect. In total, Paula made the gathering more civilized and sanitary, and for that we are in her debt.

Some of you may be aware that my eldest child, Anne, was in town recently to get her eyes fixed by the inestimable Dr. David Harris. Per usual, he once again worked a miracle, causing the blind to see. I'm thinking to suggest he open up an affiliate practice to cause the lame to walk.

Upon seeing Paula (who runs David's practice for him) it occurred to me that I had been responsible for no less than six (vi) separate surgical procedures by David, most of which I paid for. Noting my deep involvement in the volume of his practice and my unbridled loyalty, I suggested to Paula that I just might have become eligible for a toaster-oven. She replied brusquely: "We are not a bank."
I thought quietly to myself: "I'm not either."

On Sunday, Paula, working through the good agency of Gervis, presented me with my very own toaster...admittedly a close approximation to a toaster-oven. Imagine my joy and surprise.

Although initially confounded by the abrupt change of heart by my Preferred Medical Services Provider, it finally occurred to me that the toaster rewards program must a direct result of the reforms precipitated by The Patient Protection and Affordable Care Act of 2010 (PPACA), otherwise known as Obama Care.

My annual health insurance premiums under Obama Care dropped by almost $1000.00, and now THIS! Is America GREAT, or what? I am already gleaming the 10,535 page of regulations associated with the Act, to determine the reward for seven (vii) procedures. I'm betting it's a NEW CAR! If that is the case, I will be soliciting for optical patients for referral to David this Friday, August 1, 2014 at LUNCH (DINNER) at Jason's Deli on Cumberland Avenue beginning promptly at 11:44 o'clock AM.

If you need to see better, or even if you would like to look better, please see me before going anywhere else. Daddy needs a new convertible...

Wise Word 45

In response to the most recent reminder memo, more than a few of you were happy to correct me, noting that there have been several occasions in the past when girly-women have joined us at LUNCH (DINNER). I am not too proud to admit that highly technical error, and apologize to the readers. Irregardless, I note that no one took exception to my description of the ham-fisted eating habits of Messers Woodson and Armbrister.

To be fair, until last week, it had never occurred to me that accuracy or even truthfulness were expected qualities of the reminder memos. I now know that first rate journalism demands scrupulous research and devotion to detail. I intend to do better.

I note that many well-respected publications will regularly include an *errata* section, to correct inadvertent mistakes found in prior issues. I embrace that practice. As a result, I have scoured through the earlier LUNCH (DINNER) memos to insure that the appropriate standards of truth and accuracy have been met, and find that a few minor corrections/revisions are in order;

1. In my missive of May 16, 2009, I reported that veteran Americana guitarist El Kabong would be joining the backup band for Tony Bennett's pending US tour. That information was wrong, likely caused by a defective or misread press release. We regret the error.

2. In October, 2007, when waxing on about the history of bullfighting, I misspelled Francisco Romero's name when describing his monumental contribution to the evolution of the sport. Actually, the correct spelling of his name is "Clyde Bowelwater". We apologize to the late Mr. Romero, and to his surviving family members for the error.

3. Earlier this year I reported to you about John Rodgers' success in securing his instrument-only pilot's license, and the joy of his new hobby of pleasure flights between the South American paradise of Columbia and rural landing strips of southern Florida. Thanks to the rather pointed explanation from of a couple of burly gentlemen with decidedly unpleasant dispositions, I now am very aware that the reporting was totally without foundation in fact, and that I do not know, and have never met John Rodgers. If fact, I deny any knowledge of any earlier missive. I had nothing to do with it. Grainger must

have written it. He needs to step up and take responsibility at the earliest convenience.

Based on the scrutiny of last week, I remain confident that any additional *errata* that remain overlooked will be identified by those present at LUNCH (DINNER) this Friday, August 8, 2014, at 11:51 o'clock AM, at Jason's Deli on leisurely Cumberland Avenue.

In addition to fine dining and invigorating conversation, you will be enlightened by a review of Ken Wise's latest volume, *Hiking Trails of the Great Smoky Mountains, 2nd Edition,* which was released earlier last month. Copies may be purchased on Amazon.com, and at finer stores everywhere...as well as at several ordinary stores. Buy a satchel full, as they make great Labor Day gifts.

Wise Word 46

Well...it has now been a couple of weeks since election day, and all seems to be settling out nicely, just as our founding fathers expected: a time when our communities' best and brightest step up to selflessly give back to the community.

But, of course, it doesn't work unless each and every one of the citizenry carry out their solemn duty to vote, vote, vote, as many times as possible. I take great comfort in knowing that each of you did your duty and not only voted, but voted for the right person, each time.

Voting is a responsibility that cannot be taken lightly, for it is the single protection that distinguishes us from tyrannical despots hungry for power in perpetuity.

But for the power of the ballot box, we could very easily find ourselves in the same terrible circumstance as modern day North Korean or late 20th century Haiti, where political power is handed down from father to son like a royal entitlement, with no regard for competence or concern for the the better good of the community.
Huzzah and hooray for the ballot box...absolute evidence that we are smarter than THOSE people.

You will have an opportunity to tell your favorite voter fraud story tomorrow at LUNCH (DINNER) at 11:48 o'clock AM at Jason's Deli on Cumberland Ave., nestled discretely amongst about 14,000 freshly scrubbed coeds.
Parking in the rear.

Due to the outstanding organizational efforts and skills of our own Coach Butch (our guy, not the other guy) this has proved to be an interesting week. A total of eight (8) youngsters made it to the inaugural Guys Night Out last evening. When you add that to the five (5) who mistakenly showed up Tuesday night, it has to be considered a major success.

Brother Ken was so confused by Coach Butch's emails that he showed up both nights, only to report that he hated the movie on Tuesday, and liked it even less on Wednesday. Evidently, he understood the name of the film to be " Furry", and assumed it was an animated Disney feature.

The time/date confusion continues to impact our lives. I received a testy phone call at 8:42 o'clock am this morning from Henry inquiring as to why no one was present at LUNCH (DINNER) at Jason's Deli. Apparently due to the Wednesday/Tuesday confusion, he concluded that Friday came on Thursday this week. The *time* differential, however, is inexplicable, and must be laid at Henry's feet, rather than Butch's.

Irregardless, we will convene once again tomorrow (Friday) at 11:53 o'clock AM for LUNCH (DINNER) at lovely Jason's Deli on Cumberland Avenue. A collection will be taken to purchase Butch a pocket calendar. Please be generous and prompt.

Wise Word 47

Driving to work last week, I found I was being tailgated by a small minivan of unknown provenance. I wasn't too trouble by the matter, since I did not feel particularly threatened.

The car followed me onto Henley Street and pulled in behind me in the turn lane to Church Ave., still a little uncomfortably close.

While waiting for the light to change, I looked into the rear view mirror just to see if it was a male or female driver. (I will leave it to you to divine my expectation).
Imagine my surprise to find that the guy driving was playing a trumpet, with the bell facing directly into the windshield. There was no one else in the car, and the guy was just playing his lungs out.

When the light changed and we pulled away, he dropped his left hand to steer, and kept right on playing until he left me at Walnut Street. I wanted to turn and follow him, just to get the story, but one-way streets denied me the opportunity.
The story is, I suppose, pointless, but amazing to me nonetheless. The best I can figure is that his radio had stopped working, and he was making do with the resources at his disposal.

If you have an alternate explanation, you are encouraged to share it tomorrow at LUNCH (DINNER) at Jason's Deli at 11:47 o'clock AM

Wise Word 48

In order to abate any inhibitions on attendance, I have been authorized to advise that there will be absolutely NO solicitations for the Capital Campaign at LUNCH (DINNER) tomorrow at Jason's Deli at 11:56 0'clock AM. Come enjoy a respite from the rabble.

I have no valid recollection of how it began, but the Friday LUNCHes have been carrying on for what seems like forever...10 years or more? Beats me.

During the course of those years much has been learned about our colleges over bad sandwiches and poor conversation. But...much remains to be learned, for we are complex creatures. For instance, one of our ensemble evidently believes that car keys float...amazing.

This week we are introducing a new contest. The first one to correctly identify and call out the misinformed colleague will receive a $65.00 gift certificate redeemable at Watson's Department Store located on the fab, modern Market Square Mall.

The winner will be announced tomorrow at LUNCH (DINNER) at Jason's Deli, at 11:59 o'clock AM. Enter as often as you like, as the outcome is fully rigged.

Wise Word 49

Due to the unwieldy number of our LUNCH (DINNER) colleagues, only the ten (10) highest polling members will be permitted sit at the primary table at LUNCH (DINNER) at Jason's Deli today. Those polling at 11th and lower in the most recent Rasmussen Poll are delegated to the "Happy Hour Table" situated at the back of the room, nearest the bathrooms and mop station.

Please come early (around 11:49 o'clock am) in order to find the table best suited to your status. If you are unsure of your current standing in the polls, check with the Polling Status Coordinator

Wise Word 50

In recent days there has been rather animated complaints about the quality of the programs presented at the weekly LUNCH (DINNER), and it would appear that the complaints are well taken.

The quality began deteriorating when the Chairman of our Program Committee, Ed Peterson, moved to Louisiana several months ago.

The Oversight Committee appointed a sub-committee to reach out to the Program Chair to see what could be done to remedy the situation. The efforts of the Sub-Committee for Program Oversight have been largely without benefit, primarily because the Program Committee Chairman left no forwarding address, and upon departing for Louisiana left instructions that no one associated with LUNCH (DINNER) was to ever attempt to contact him again.

Pending the final Report of the Sub-Committee on Program Oversight, I have generously agreed to take responsibility for this weeks program, which will feature an exposition of photos of my new grand babies. The formal program will last approximately 90 minutes, after which time I will be happy to entertain questions.
You do not want to miss this fascinating presentation. I am certainly looking forward to it.

The program begins promptly at 11:48 o'clock AM at Jason's Deli located in the crime-free Cumberland Avenue Strip

And Some Wise Aphorisms

Wise Aphorism 1

The scheduled topic for discussion will be an analysis of the shopworn adage to quote put your best foot forward", and the related but distinct direction of the Godfather of soul to "do it on the good foot."

The two specific queries to be pursued are: 1. what visual and tactile evidence may one rely upon in determining which is the best for good foot; and 2. what are the implications of these two instructions for a three legged dog?

Wise Aphorism 2

The scheduled topic for discussion is: short track speed skating (HOOHEE) including specifically the career of the great Olympic gold medalist Apollo Ohno, and his ongoing efforts to preserve and promote the music of the late John Lennon.

Wise Aphorism 3

The scheduled topic for discussion: Roomba robot vacuum cleaners: (a) a modern engineering marvel that will lessen the drudgery of happy housewife everywhere; or (b) just plain creepy.

Wise Aphorism 4

the scheduled topic for discussion is: the recent proposal of the UT athletics department to rebrand all distaff sports programs to the "Vols" and rebrand all men's programs to the "Gentleman Vols."

Wise Aphorism 5

The scheduled topic for discussion will be the dialect influences of Popeye the sailor man.

Wise Aphorism 6

The scheduled topic for discussion is dog training. Is it—a true science, an art, magic, sophistry, or imaginary. Be prepared to defend your position.

Wise Aphorism 7

the scheduled topic for discussion is the substitution of the phrase "no problem" for the classic "you're welcome" in reply to thank you. Where would Emily post stand on the issue?

Wise Aphorism 8

The scheduled topic for discussion will be structured as a formal debate, with the following: "RESOLVED," the tomfoolery is a greater threat to the social fabric of modern American society than horseplay."

Their latest license plate on Monday Wednesday or Friday shall argue the affirmative. Those who Social Security number ends in a positive number shall argue the negative. Prepare accordingly.

Wise Aphorism 9

At the harried request of one of our members, the scheduled topic for discussion is identifying and developing remedies for canine cognitive dysfunction!

You are implored to bring your best ideas. Food will be served for a modest fee.

Wise Aphorism 10

periodically it is incumbent to ponder the imponderable, and such will be the task of the scheduled topic of discussion: in what state is *Hooverville* located?

Arguments must be supported by evidence from either Green Acres or petticoat Junction.

Also bring your best Alabama joke. Mine— we should be grateful to Alabama for the invention of the toothbrush. We know it was invented in that state, otherwise it would be called a teeth brush.

Wise Aphorism 11

The scheduled topic for discussion will be an analysis of the quality and vitality of the discussions at the immediate past three lunch meetings. You won't want to miss it.

Wise Aphorism 12

The scheduled topic for discussion is: "food poisoning— is it real or just the imagination running amuck?" Personal anecdotes will be welcomed, especially if in the form of a limerick.

Wise Aphorism 13

The scheduled topic for discussion will be the proposed legislation that would prohibit reaching for discussion of confefy is at historic black colleges and universities.

Wise Aphorism 14

The scheduled topic for discussion is: Friggatriskaidekaphobia. Do your best.

Wise Aphorism 15

The scheduled topic for discussion will be Bernie Madoff, but only because I've been watching a documentary about him. An amazingly bad person.

Wise Aphorism 16

The scheduled topic for discussion: "What traits, characteristics, and skills qualify the toucan to be the image and spokesbird for *Froot Loops?* I'm prepared.

Wise Aphorism 17

In compliance with mandates from the US Department of Education, are scheduled topic for discussion will be: "Harry, formerly known as Prince, and Megan, the Princess bride." Specifically, discussion will be directed toward the efficacy of a scorched earth strategy in the resolution of family disputes. Please remember that your comments may be recorded for training purposes.

Wise Aphorism 18

The scheduled topic for discussion will be: "Birds— real or just an urban myth?"

Wise Aphorism 19

The scheduled topic for discussion will be: "the employment o ellipses (...) And text messages... Is it a. An effective tool to segregate pithy points... (ii) a petty annoyance... (4) evidence of arrogant condescension... or (c) the bane of modern social communication?" Be prepared to defend your position with real-life examples.

Wise Aphorism 20

Prognosticators, forecasters and pendants dominate the unscripted media, whether on the all-news cable channels, radio call-in shows, the Storm Team Action Report, ESPN talk shows, or the sports page of any newspaper. Augury and weighted predictions overwhelm our media and social interactions. Hence the scheduled topic for discussion is, "Prophesy— does it have a future?" It is predicted that you must attend to be heard.

Wise Aphorism 21

The scheduled topic for discussion will follow a law school exam format

ASSUME that you have been indicted on multiple felony charges, the evidence of which is abundant and compelling. Query: which of the following absurdist characteristics would you least prefer to have as a co-defendant/co-conspirator or: Moe of the Three Stooges; Gilligan of desert isle thing; or Rudy Giuliani, America's Mayor?"

Wise Aphorism 22

We have been informed that the staff responsible for preparing and publishing your weekly reminder notice about lunch on Friday at 12 o'clock noon at the Fieldhouse Social has joined the Hollywood writers strike. As a result you should not expect to receive a reminder notice this week and there will be no properly advertised topic of discussion. These are perilous times. Happily, we are advised that attending lunch on Friday will not be deemed a scab action so you can proceed to lunch with all dispatch. Power to the worker!!

Wise Aphorism 23

Please be advised that lunch has been deemed an essential function and will proceed to per usual even in the event of a government shutdown. In an effort to remain engaged in current events, the scheduled topic for discussion will be the casual connection between the looming government shutdown and Hillary's missing emails.

Wise Aphorism 24

The scheduled topic for discussion will combine a study of the dynamic societal role of non-verbal communication with the most compelling local issue ripped from the pages of the news Sentinel: "Knoxville's Missing Middle Finger— what are we going to do about it?"

—Sort Of